The
Daily Rounds
of
a Hound

To Asher & Ella, Enjoy your adventures with "The Hound!" Ed Payne

Written by Ed Payne

Illustrated by Britt Sekulic

ISBN: 0615758312
ISBN-13: 978-0615758312

DEDICATION

This book is dedicated to my wife and girls -- Laura, Ellyce, Corynne and, of course, Molly Malone -- who all helped inspire this book.
- Ed

I dedicate this book to my husband Mirko and to all the people that are fearful of making that first step in a career change. This is proof that "Yes, you can."
- Britt

Consider the hound.
Just for a minute or two.

Don't think too hard.
Be she tan or red or brown,
consider the hound.

What is she thinking?

What is she doing?

Where is she going?
Consider the hound.

Consider.

Just consider...

The daily rounds of a hound.

There's patrolling the house.

There's protecting the kids.

There are so many missions --
and some of them hid.

What's that smell?

Molly is -- well, we're not quite sure --
a dog of a special line.

Is she spaniel, lab or setter?
Well, yes and no or maybe something better.

Maybe she's a Kooikerhondje?
But oh what is that?

And can you really find
a Dutch decoy dog
in a place like that?

What place you ask?
That's a fair question, I'd say.
Our hound Molly --
Molly Malone to be exact --
we found at the pound.

A shelter dog is what our hound is.
A dog with a special story,
but one we'll never know.

Did she live with rich folks

or poor?

We asked Molly once,
but mum's the word.
So we made up our own,
one that's never been heard.
Molly's Irish we're sure.
She's red and white --
that's our clue.

And we need
to tell you
something else,
she came with
puppies too.

Our hound came with pups --
nine stowaways to be exact.
Now who would have
expected that?
They came quite soon,
just a few weeks later.
A shock to be sure,
but still quite a treasure.

Yipping and yapping
they grew up quite quick.

They all went to new homes lickity split.

Yes, Molly has a story.
One we're sure is quite swell.
But as we all know,
ladies don't kiss and tell.

So, consider the hound --
our hound Molly Malone.
And once again,
consider the rounds of a hound.

Sleeping, snacking,
possibly learning a new trick,
she has lots of things to do,
maybe chasing a stick.

But Molly is mellow,
chasing sticks won't do.
She doesn't even bark --
not more than a time or two.

Sleeping is good,
finding a comfortable spot.
Maybe following family
members around

or finding a cool place to lie
when it's hot.

One last time, consider the hound --
your own Molly Malone.
And please consider the rounds of your hound.

Your hound may be different --
a lot different for sure.
But whether collie, bulldog or Mexican hairless --
or some special mix in between --

love that hound,
tan, red or brown,
and you'll get more
in return
you'll see.

MOLLY MALONE

ACKNOWLEDGEMENTS

We would like to give a special thanks to Chelsea J. Carter for seeing our potential and bringing us together creatively. Without her, this book would not have been possible.

Thank you to my mom, Carolynn Clarida, who encouraged me to take the manuscript out of the drawer and let "The Hound" roam. Thank you to Victoria Wilcox, Phil Gast, Emerson Cochran, Martha Lee Sanders and Lea Longley.
- Ed

Thank you Corrie Pappas for inspiring me to try another side of my creativity. Thank you to my husband Mirko for his discerning eye, fun ideas and blatant honesty on this project. Thank you to my family for their enthusiasm and support. Thank you to my clients for their fierce loyalty and encouragement.
- Britt

Thank you to all our Kickstarter supporters:

Aimee Ahmed	Judy Akin
Amity Beard	Katie McMahon
Anjanette Levert	Kelly Duncan
Ben Persons	Lynne Earls
Carolynn Utiger Clarida	Marianne Bentley
Catherine Shoichet	Martha Johnson
Chelsea J. Carter	Matt & Liz Harper
Chris Lin	Michael Barmish
Corrie Pappas	Michelle
Dan Edmonds	Michelle Drak
Debbie Bontrager	Michelle La Caille Faldoski
George Sekulich	Patrick Baird Patty Jane
Greg D'Avis	Polly Wilson
Irena Petrovic	Radmila Sekulic
Jane E. Burwell	Scott Collette
Jay. S. Hergott	Staley Robertson
Jean Marie Shiraldi	Suzanne Austin
Jeanine Todd	Suzi Kljajic
Jennifer Noble	Tammy Stephens
Jill Davis	Tracie Miller
Joanna Siegla	Troy Todd
John Benjamin Brumfield	Wendy Cope
John Ford	Winston Carter
Joyce Murray	

ABOUT THE AUTHOR

Ed Payne is a veteran journalist with 30 years in the business, the last two decades at CNN. His stories appear on CNN.com and you'll often hear his voice on TV reports for the network and on hundreds of affiliates across the United States. "The Daily Rounds of a Hound" is not only his first book, but also his first children's book, although his journalistic endeavors have been read by millions of people around the world.

Made in the USA
Charleston, SC
08 September 2014